W9-AZQ-021

Randall Reindeer™
Naughty and Nice Report!

Copyright © 2010 Dalmatian Press, LLC
All rights reserved
Printed in Mexico

Published by Piggy Toes Press,
an imprint of Dalmatian Publishing Group
Atlanta, GA 30329

Creative, editorial and design by Dorothea DePrisco, Jenna Riggs and Susan Reagan
in coordination with Dalmatian Press 2010.

No part of this book may be reproduced or copied in any form
without the written permission of Piggy Toes Press.

ISBN: 1-61524-365-8 • RRD36206

Randall Reindeer™
Naughty and Nice Report!

Randall Reindeer's Naughty and Nice Report is about Randall,
an eager and loyal reindeer who wishes to save the day
when Santa loses the Naughty and Nice List!

Randall Reindeer had big dreams.

More than anything, he wanted a special job at Santa's Castle. While Randall was a great listener, and an even better helper, his enthusiasm always seemed to cause problems. Randall's first job out was assistant to the Reindeer Team. But still, Randall dreamed of doing more.

For example, one snowy morning Vixen was running late. Randall quickly grabbed Vixen's spot. But, he got tangled in the reins.

He caused such a ruckus that the reindeer lost control of the sleigh; the reindeer crashed, while Randall slowly floated down to a pile of soft snow.

That day, Randall was assigned to another job.

The next day, Randall started his new job in the workshop.

Only, Randall broke some of the toys while trying to fix them.
Then, he somehow got himself tied up with the laces on his elf shoes.
And to top it off, the elf hat that was part of his uniform was so big;
Randall could barely see what he was doing.

That day, Randall was assigned to yet another job.

Randall's new job was to help Mrs. Claus bake cookies. The kitchen phone rang. Mrs. Claus whispered, "Yes, we've lost the entire list. Santa and I are going to have to figure out a solution and FAST!"

"OH NO! NOT THE LIST! They can't find the Naughty and Nice List!" Randall ran to find his buddy, Timmy.

While the other elves were busy decorating Christmas trees, Timmy was sitting on the ice, drawing pictures in the snow.

Timmy was not the most magical of elves but he was a wonderful artist. Timmy's biggest dream was to paint Santa's portrait for Christmas.

Randall came running up to him and said, "Come on, Timmy, quick!" The two friends ran to Randall's stall in the reindeer barn. Randall told Timmy that the Naughty and Nice List was missing.

"I can hear you gentlemen, and you are ruining my beauty sleep!" yelled someone from across the barn.

"Oh, Camilla, stop eavesdropping and help us!" said Timmy.

Camilla was a small arctic hare with beautiful white fur. She was very smart but extremely lazy. Stretching, Camilla said, "Goodness Randall, you fly don't you? This is your chance!

Get yourself down there and make a new list!"

Randall said, "Yes! Yes! I will get Santa everything he needs! I'll save the day!"

Camilla, Timmy, and Randall made a plan for Randall to fly down to the children of the world. Camilla gave Randall a map and a compass. Timmy gave Randall a messenger bag and some naughty and nice report cards that he'd typed up.

Randall took off running. He caught the breeze and was airborne! He waved to his friends, "WEEE!" he squealed with happiness.

Finally, after several hours, Randall made a smooth landing and thanks to Timmy's elf magic he was much smaller than usual. This made it very easy for him to keep out of sight in each home.

He had to learn where to hide so he could start his special Christmas duties.

In the first home, he sat on a lamp but it was too warm. Ouch!

In second home, he sat on the cat's bed, but it was already occupied.

In the third home, he tried the kitchen, but whoops, he landed straight in the salad bowl!

After Randall found the right places to hide, he began listening to see who was naughty, and who was nice.

Randall enjoyed sitting in each house.

Some families sang Christmas carols. Some families adorned their homes with brightly colored lights and homemade decorations.

Some families simply enjoyed reading Christmas stories.

When Randall saw a child sharing or doing a good deed, he could feel the Christmas spirit tingle inside his little reindeer heart. He loved seeing children sharing and being kind.

It made Randall sad to see children being unkind or to see them pouting. When a child was naughty, Randall felt sad.

At the end of each day, Randall would leave a report card, letting each child know what he'd observed and telling them if they'd been acting naughty or nice.

Back at the North Pole, Timmy was watching the weather report. A blizzard was approaching! Timmy rushed to call Randall, but there was no answer.

It was Christmas Eve, and time to return to the North Pole. Unfortunately, Randall was so excited that he left his compass behind.

As Randall flew by Jack Frost's castle inside a fluffy snow cloud, he lost his balance.

And then...WHOOSH!

Randall was taken by a mighty wind! His map flew out of his bag. He was rolling around the sky and couldn't find his compass!

Just as Randall was on a downward
spiral toward the icy tower of Jack Frost's
castle, he heard the cheery sound of jingle bells!

The snow blocked his view, but he felt something large
but gentle pick him up. It was Santa!

Santa said in a kind voice, "All of Santa's helpers check
the weather before takeoff. We'd better get you the proper
help for next year!"

Randall beamed with pride. He had found
a new job!

When the sleigh landed, everyone cheered for Randall. Santa announced, "Attention, everyone! Randall, Timmy, and Camilla saved Christmas! Next year, Randall will visit the homes of children around the world and report back with the Naughty and Nice List!"

Then Santa whispered to Timmy, "I would be honored to have you paint my portrait!" Timmy glowed with joy.

Are you ready for Christmas? Have you been naughty, or nice?

When the winter winds start to blow and you are getting ready for Santa to come, be sure to be on your best behavior!

Merry Christmas!

Randall Reindeer's Top Ten Favorite Christmas Traditions

10. Decorating the many Christmas Trees at the North Pole.
9. Helping the elves get all the toys ready for the girls and boys.
8. Singing Christmas Carols with all the other reindeer.
7. Helping Mrs. Claus bake her famous cookies.
6. Getting out the Christmas Countdown Calendar with his parents.
5. Writing a letter to Santa (yes even reindeers have to send in their toy requests!)
4. Drinking hot chocolate and getting to stay up extra late on Christmas Eve.
3. Helping to clean and polish Santa's sleigh to get it ready for his big trip on Christmas Eve.
2. Exchanging presents with his best friends Timmy and Camilla.
1. Being in charge of the naughty and nice list for Santa.

Now make a list of your ten favorite Christmas traditions! Create a new list every year and keep them with Randall then you can see how much they change from year to year.

Mrs. Claus' Recipes For Santa's Favorite Cookies

Peanut Butter Cookies

Ingredients:
½ cup peanut butter
¼ cup butter
½ cup brown sugar
½ cup granulated sugar
1 egg, well beaten
1 cup sifted all-purpose flour
1 tsp baking soda.

Directions:
1. Preheat oven to 350º.
2. Cream peanut butter and butter together. Add sugar gradually, continuing to cream until mixture is light and fluffy.
3. Add beaten egg. Sift flour and baking soda together and mix.
4. Drop mixture, one tsp at a time on cookie sheet.
5. Bake 10-15 minutes

Makes 4 dozen cookies*

*Santa thinks these are best with a glass of chocolate milk.

Cookies and Cream Truffles

Ingredients:
1 package cream cheese, softened
1 package cream filled chocolate sandwich cookies, crushed
2 packages semi-sweet chocolate, melted

Directions:
1. Mix crushed cookies with cream cheese until mixed.
2. Shape into 1 inch balls and place on cookie sheet.
3. Dip balls in melted chocolate.
4. Refrigerate until firm.

Makes 48 truffles*

*Santa Loves these with Hot Cocoa

Sugar Cookies

Ingredients:
½ pound butter
1 cup sugar
2 eggs
1 tbsp water
1 tsp vanilla extract
1 tsp baking powder
2.5 cups flour

Directions:
1. Preheat oven to 400.
2. Cream butter and sugar together with a wooden spoon. Beat eggs until very light and add to creamed mixture, beat well and add water and vanilla extract.
3. Add baking powder to ½ cup flour and sift into other ingredients. Beat until light and then add remaining 2 cups of flour and mix thoroughly.
4. Roll thinly on floured baking board and cut out with cookie cutter.
5. Bake for 10 minutes.

Makes 50 cookies*

Santa likes these warm with a glass of milk

Chocolate Chip Cookies

Ingredients:
½ cup butter
½ cup sugar
¼ cup brown sugar, packed
1 egg
1 tsp vanilla
1 cup flour
½ tsp baking soda
½ tsp salt
1 cup chocolate chips

Directions:
1. Preheat oven to 375
2. Mix butter, sugar, brown sugar, egg and vanilla until mixed. Blend in dry ingredients
3. Stir in chocolate chips.
4. Place on ungreased cookie sheet, 2 inches apart.
5. Bake for 8-10 minutes.

Makes about 4 dozen cookies

Santa likes these with ice cold milk

Reindeer Love:

1. Fresh Carrots

2. Apple Slices

3. Sugar Cubes

4. Pretzels (yes a true reindeer favorite)

5. Chocolate Candy (but only in moderation)

Randall's Favorite Holiday Songs

Up on the Housetop
(a song about Randall's reindeer friends)

Up on the housetop reindeer pause
Out jumps good old Santa Claus
Down through the chimney with lots of toys
All for the little ones, Christmas joys
Ho, ho ho! Who wouldn't go?
Ho, ho ho! Who wouldn't go?

Up on the housetop, click, click, click
Down through the chimney with old Saint Nick

First comes the stocking of little Nell
Oh, dear Santa fill it well
Give her a dolly that laughs and cries
One that will open and shut her eyes
Ho, ho, ho! Who wouldn't go?
Ho, ho, ho! Who wouldn't go?

Up on the housetop, click, click, click
Down through the chimney with old Saint Nick

Next comes the stocking of little Will
Oh, just see what a glorious fill
Here is a hammer and lots of tacks
Also a ball and a whip that cracks
Ho, ho ho! Who wouldn't go?
Ho, ho, ho! Who wouldn't go?

Up on the housetop, click, click, click
Down through the chimney with old Saint Nick

We wish you a Merry Christmas
(a song of holiday merriment)

We wish you a merry Christmas

We wish you a Merry Christmas;
We wish you a Merry Christmas;
We wish you a Merry Christmas and a Happy New Year.
Good tidings we bring to you and your kin;
Good tidings for Christmas and a Happy New Year.

Oh, bring us a figgy pudding;
Oh, bring us a figgy pudding;
Oh, bring us a figgy pudding and a cup of good cheer
We won't go until we get some;
We won't go until we get some;
We won't go until we get some, so bring some out here

We wish you a Merry Christmas;
We wish you a Merry Christmas;
We wish you a Merry Christmas and a Happy New Year.

Jingle Bells
(a song about Christmas fun!)

Dashing through the snow	Oh, jingle bells, jingle bells
In a one horse open sleigh	Jingle all the way
O'er the fields we go	Oh, what fun it is to ride
Laughing all the way	In a one horse open sleigh
Bells on bob tails ring	Jingle bells, jingle bells
Making spirits bright	Jingle all the way
What fun it is to laugh and sing	Oh, what fun it is to ride
A sleighing song tonight	In a one horse open sleigh

Now sing some of your favorite Christmas songs!

Reindeer Report!

Child's Name:_____   Days until Christmas: _____

Naughty
☐ Being Unkind   ☐ Shouting
☐ Not Helpful   ☐ Pouting

A note from Randall:

Nice
☐ Being Kind   ☐ Sharing
☐ Helping Others   ☐ Being Honest

_____
_____
_____
_____

Reindeer Report!

Child's Name:_____   Days until Christmas: _____

Naughty
☐ Being Unkind   ☐ Shouting
☐ Not Helpful   ☐ Pouting

A note from Randall:

Nice
☐ Being Kind   ☐ Sharing
☐ Helping Others   ☐ Being Honest

Reindeer Report!

Child's Name:_____   Days until Christmas: _____

Naughty
☐ Being Unkind   ☐ Shouting
☐ Not Helpful   ☐ Pouting

A note from Randall:

Nice
☐ Being Kind   ☐ Sharing
☐ Helping Others   ☐ Being Honest

Reindeer Report!

Child's Name:_____   Days until Christmas: _____

Naughty
☐ Being Unkind   ☐ Shouting
☐ Not Helpful   ☐ Pouting

A note from Randall:

Nice
☐ Being Kind   ☐ Sharing
☐ Helping Others   ☐ Being Honest

Reindeer Report!

Child's Name:_____   Days until Christmas: _____

Naughty
☐ Being Unkind   ☐ Shouting
☐ Not Helpful   ☐ Pouting

A note from Randall:

Nice
☐ Being Kind   ☐ Sharing
☐ Helping Others   ☐ Being Honest

Reindeer Report!

Child's Name:_____   Days until Christmas: _____

Naughty
☐ Being Unkind   ☐ Shouting
☐ Not Helpful   ☐ Pouting

A note from Randall:

Nice
☐ Being Kind   ☐ Sharing
☐ Helping Others   ☐ Being Honest

Reindeer Report!

Child's Name:_____   Days until Christmas: _____

Naughty
☐ Being Unkind   ☐ Shouting
☐ Not Helpful   ☐ Pouting

A note from Randall:

Nice
☐ Being Kind   ☐ Sharing
☐ Helping Others   ☐ Being Honest

Reindeer Report!

Child's Name:_____   Days until Christmas: _____

Naughty
☐ Being Unkind   ☐ Shouting
☐ Not Helpful   ☐ Pouting

A note from Randall:

Nice
☐ Being Kind   ☐ Sharing
☐ Helping Others   ☐ Being Honest

Reindeer Report!

Child's Name:_____   Days until Christmas: _____

Naughty
☐ Being Unkind   ☐ Shouting
☐ Not Helpful   ☐ Pouting

A note from Randall:

Nice
☐ Being Kind   ☐ Sharing
☐ Helping Others   ☐ Being Honest

Reindeer Report!

Child's Name:_____   Days until Christmas: _____

Naughty
☐ Being Unkind   ☐ Shouting
☐ Not Helpful   ☐ Pouting

A note from Randall:

Nice
☐ Being Kind   ☐ Sharing
☐ Helping Others   ☐ Being Honest